THIS BOOK BELONGS TO:
_____

READ ISLAND

To Silas, my little man of the forest
- N.M.

To Tobyn, my book-loving boy
- A.F.

ABOUT THIS BOOK

The illustrations for this book were drawn by hand and rendered digitally. This book was edited by Sandy Ferguson Fuller and Bethany Strout. Art direction and design was by Sasha Illingworth. The display text was set in Adobe Garamond Pro, and the display type was hand-lettered by Alice Feagan. This book was printed in North Mankato, Minnesota on paper from responsible sources.

FSC
www.fsc.org
MIX
Paper from
responsible sources
FSC® C008080

READ ISLAND

READ ISLAND

WRITTEN BY
NICOLE MAGISTRO

ILLUSTRATED BY
ALICE FEAGAN

There is a place beneath the stars
That welcomes friends from near and far.
Just after dawn, the sun peeks through.
The mighty sea makes way for you.

Past rocky cliffs and cozy nooks,
You'll find an island made of books.

A sea wolf howls. Her lilting cry
Is like a soothing lullaby.
Every creature knows that sound –
They know it's safe to come around.

Each one comes here for story time,
For books with pictures, prose, and rhyme.

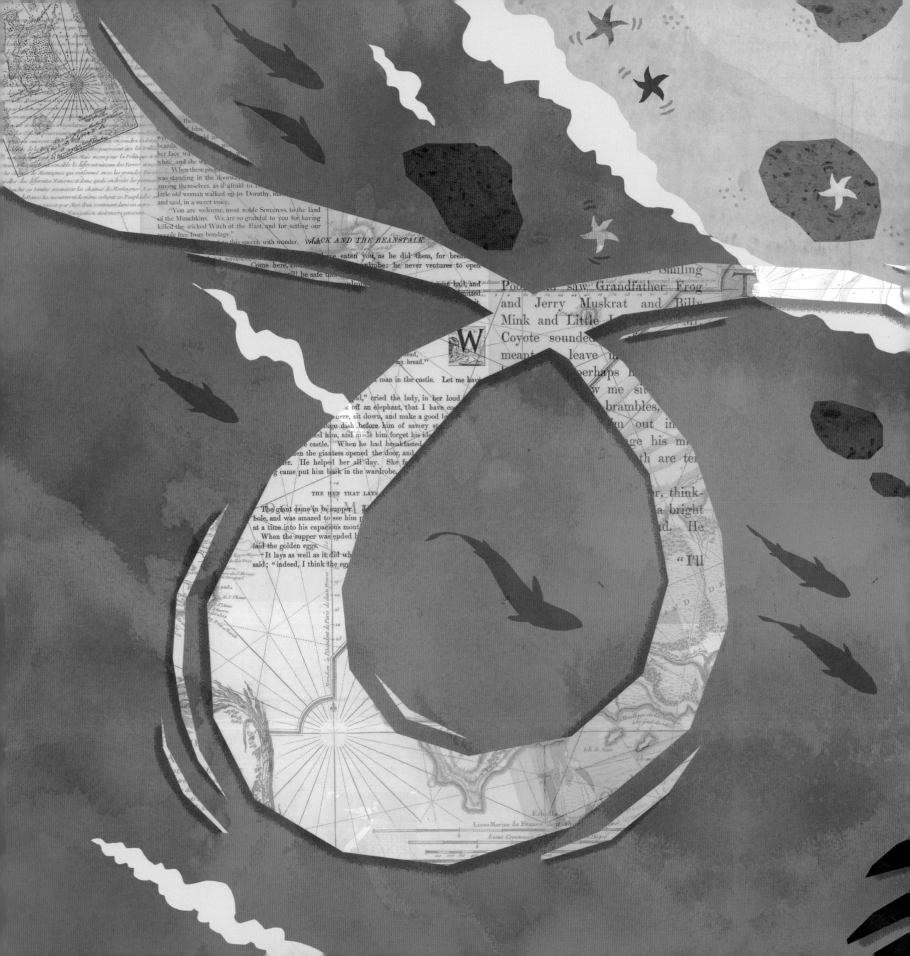

Starfish dance and salmon reign.
The raven circles his domain.

A grizzly lumbers from her cave.

An eagle lands,

a humpback waves.

A moose sniffs at the salty air.

Who comes now?

Rare spirit bear.

From high up in the snowy peaks,
A gang of elk can hear wolf speak.
Cascading downhill, young and old,
Quick – before the tale unfolds.

Now fox arrives with cougar, mouse,
And butterflies to fill the house.
Joyfully they congregate,
Circling in to celebrate.

Can you join them?
Just be still.
Breathe in.
Breathe out.
Listen well.

Relax, observe, explore, let's go!
Remember this, a story flows.

From out to in, from here to there –
Books can take you anywhere.

To the city, into space,
To a very quiet place,
To a rainbow reaching high,
To the deepest darkest sky.

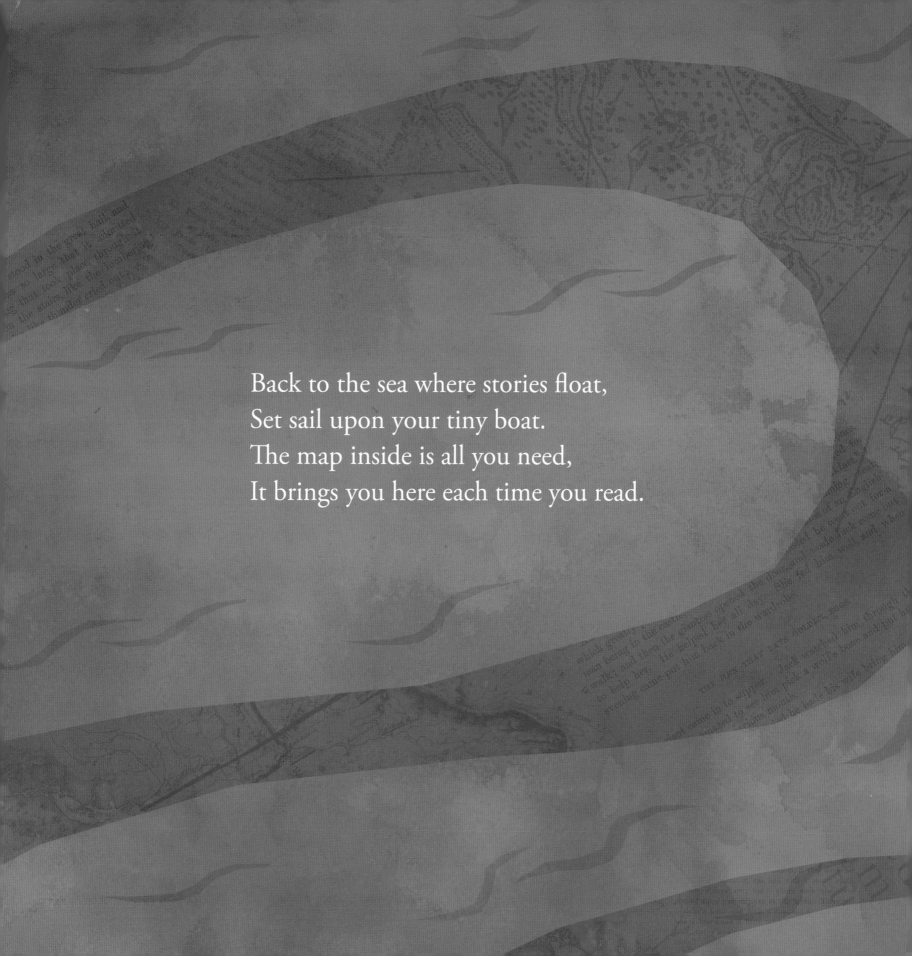

Back to the sea where stories float,
Set sail upon your tiny boat.
The map inside is all you need,
It brings you here each time you read.

For make-believe though it may look,
There is an island made of books.
This world of stories, safe and true,
Is always here to welcome you.

Be still.
Breathe out, then in again,
And listen for your island friends.